Chibt
G4631an-wo
Glass, Andrew 1949-
The Wondrous Whirligig /
the Wright Brothers' first
SUN 1064438557 NOV

WITHDRAWN

WORN SOILED, OBSOLETE

D0633299

The WONDROUS WHIRLIGIG

THE WRIGHT BROTHERS' FIRST FLYING MACHINE

ANDREW GLASS

HOLIDAY HOUSE / NEW YORK

To Joann

"We were lucky to grow up where there was always
much encouragement to investigate whatever aroused curiosity."
—ORVILLE WRIGHT

Copyright © 2003 by Andrew Glass
All Rights Reserved
Printed in the United States of America
www.holidayhouse.com
First Edition

LIBRARY OF CONGRESS CATALOGING-IN-PUBLICATION DATA
Glass, Andrew, 1949–
The wondrous whirligig: the Wright Brothers' first flying machine / Andrew Glass.—1st ed.
p. cm.
Summary: Inspired by a model helicopter and encouraged by their parents and sister,
young Orville and Wilbur Wright attempt to build a life-size helicopter from scrap.
ISBN 0-8234-1717-4
1. Wright, Orville, 1871–1948—Childhood and youth—Juvenile fiction. 2. Wright, Wilbur, 1867–1912—
Childhood and youth—Juvenile fiction. [1. Wright, Orville, 1871–1948—Childhood and youth—Juvenile fiction.
2. Wright, Wilbur, 1867–1912—Childhood and youth—Fiction. 3. Helicopters—Fiction.
4. Flight—Fiction. 5. Inventors—Fiction] I. Title
PZ7.G48115 Wo 2003
[Fic]—dc21   2002068940

Papa was a traveling preacher. Sometimes he surprised us with a gift he'd purchased in a distant city, a picture book or a puzzle wrapped in brown paper. But one particular morning, when I was seven years old, Papa came home with a special present.

"Look what I've brought you boys!" he said. "A wondrous whirligig."

Papa turned one propeller around and around until the elastic band was tightly twisted into knots. "Behold!" he said, and spread his hands wide. The spinning whirligig gyrated, zigzagging dangerously above lace doilies in our dark parlor.

It bumped the ceiling, flip-flopped, and dropped to the carpet.

"Kerplunk!" said Kate.

"Extraordinary," said Willy. "Truly."

"It's called a helicopter," said Papa. "It was invented by a Frenchman named Mr. Penaud."

"It flies like a blind bat," I said.

"An excellent name for it," said Mother.

"And an excellent reason to fly Mr. Penaud's bat outdoors," said Papa.

Outdoors, the *Bat* spun in loopy swirls. The elastic unwound, and the *Bat* swooped, flip-flopped, and crashed.

"Peculiar," said Willy.

I suggested tying a toy soldier near the bottom propeller to balance the *Bat*. We attached some bent wire with wooden spools for wheels, so the *Bat* stood up all by itself.

Mother and little Kate came to see.

The *Bat* gyrated in tight circles. It plummeted suddenly. We held our breath.

But it bounced neatly on its springy wheels. "Whew."

"I believe you boys have tamed the *Bat*," said Mother proudly.

"Why don't we build a big bat and fly it right over Cedar Rapids?" I shouted.

"Why not indeed?" said Willy.

"Because," Papa rumbled in his deepest preacher's voice, "if the good Lord had intended folks to fly, folks would have wings like angels instead of feet like folks."

But no idea was ever too far-fetched for Mother. "Let's settle down at the kitchen table, sharpen some pencils, and puzzle it out," she said.

Papa shrugged his shoulders. "Well, my dear," he said, "I suppose the good Lord sometimes changes his mind."

Wilbur drew the *Bat*, but bigger.

"Probably it won't be so different from building a chair like the one we made out of broomsticks," I said.

"Do we still have those drawings?" asked Willy.

"Right here," I said. "Little Kate's old pram wheels would fit too, I bet."

"Excellent idea, Orv," said Willy, spreading out another piece of brown paper.

"Make sure to leave plenty of room for the bottom propeller."

"Precisely!"

Mother drew a long, double curve between the propellers. "I'm sure we can find such a handle long enough for two strong boys to crank together."

"*Muscle power!*" we shouted.

Propellers were a real predicament. "You know," said Willy, "old windmills were made of stretched fabric, just like twirling propeller kites."

We already knew how to build kites. We had plenty of kite drawings. Finally the working drawings of the *Big Bat* looked like a genuine boy-powered flying machine.

"An admirable apparatus," said Wilbur.

By the next day word spread that we were building a
flying machine. Kids climbed the fence for a better look.
Some left and came back later with little brothers and
sisters and visiting cousins.

Loren and Reuch came home hungry and impatient as usual to wash up and get right to the soup. "We are building a whirligig flying machine," Willy announced proudly.

"You don't say so," Reuch replied solemnly, looking the *Big Bat* over carefully.

"You know, Reuch," said Loren, "some fellows have little *baby* brothers."

"And what do you suppose we have, Loren?" asked Reuch.

"Little *brainy* brothers!" They laughed. That was their favorite joke.

"Yessireebob," said Loren. "Don't you boys fly off in that contraption without saying good-bye."

By the time we were ready for the *Big Bat*'s first
flight, lots of folks had heard what we were up to
and came around to see for themselves.

"Will ye looky there at that contraption."

"Bishop Wright's youngest boys are a pure stitch."

"Ain't they, though?"

Loren and Reuch returned, wearing their Sunday hats and carrying long planks joined together.

"We considered you little fellas might need a head start. So we'll just fit this ramp over that old teeter-totter and bounce your wondrous whatchamacallit right into the sky."

Papa let the screen door slam. He held two battered caps stuffed with scarves and old socks. "Put these on, boys," he ordered. "Best not to challenge the laws of nature with your bare heads."

Mother tied the lumpy hats on our heads. Loren and Reuch lifted us to the top of the long seesaw ramp. We were ready to fly.

But first Papa prayed. "Dear Lord, should you see fit to share a little space in the heavens tonight with this wondrous whirligig built by these fine boys, please grant them safe return to our good earth. Amen."

"Amen!" responded all the folks.

"Ready, set, start cranking!"

We rolled down, down the long ramp, cranking around and around as fast as we could. And as we rolled down, Loren and Reuch leaped up to the top of the ramp and catapulted us into the air. . . . "ALLEY-OOP!"

And if everything had worked just the way Willy
drew it on brown paper . . .

. . . the twirling propellers would have caught the wind. We might have ascended smoothly, whirling, cranking against the air, gyrating over hills and fields and rivers. Folks would have shaded their eyes and pointed. "What a grand enterprise," they'd surely have exclaimed. We could have circled effortlessly on the breeze, swirling back around and over our little house. Folks would have cheered, "Hurrah!" as we gently, gently descended.

Of course we were never truly airborne, not that day. In fact, even though we cranked the propellers for all we were worth, we barely bounced. We toppled right off the end of the ramp. The pram wheels snapped and the broomsticks cracked, fabric ripped, joints twisted and popped loose. The top propeller hung in jagged tatters.

Mother looked a little concerned, not surprised though and not in the least discouraged.

"Kerplunk," said little Kate clearly amid all the laughter and the hoots.

"As I suspected," said Papa. "But remember, boys, gravity is one of the Lord's blessings too."

At that very moment a man in a brown suit peddled by on a high wheeler. He waved.

"Willy," I said. "Do you think by peddling we might rotate the propellers—"

"At a sufficient speed," he interrupted.

"To lift us into the air," I said.

"A bicycle-a-gig," we shouted.

"Let's go in the kitchen and sharpen some pencils," said Wilbur.

"Not tonight, boys," said Papa. "It's getting on toward supper time. Tomorrow will come soon enough."

AUTHOR'S NOTE

BISHOP MILTON WRIGHT

SUSAN KOERNER WRIGHT

Nine days after *The New York Times* predicted that it would be a million years or so before people actually flew in machines, Orville Wright was carried into the air at Kitty Hawk, North Carolina, on the machine he and his brother Wilbur had built themselves.

I based my story on the often reported account of a gadget Bishop Wright really did bring his sons while the family was living in Cedar Rapids, Iowa, in 1878. It was a flying toy invented by Alphonse Penaud with propellers at either end and powered by strips of rubber. The basic design dated back to the time of Leonardo da Vinci. Orville named it the *Bat*. In most accounts, he and Wilbur made some improvements and built a somewhat larger version that didn't work because of its increased weight. But according to *The Bishop's Boys: A Life of Wilbur and Orville Wright* by Tom Crouch, Orville was reprimanded by his teacher in Cedar Rapids for fiddling with bits of wood in class. He explained that he was working on a machine that might enable him to fly with his brother. In the spirit of a tall tale, I built on this account while including many of the facts of their lives.

Wilbur and Orville really did build a chair made of broomsticks and a wagon and designed kites, which they sold. Their mother, Susan Koerner Wright, who often helped them, never hesitated to roll up her sleeves when something needed to be rigged up or repaired. She encouraged Orville and Wilbur to make working drawings for every project. The boys truly grew up in a warm family where, as Orville later said, imagination was never discouraged. They went on dusting themselves off and trying again until they finally constructed a machine in 1903 that carried Orville into the sky for twelve seconds.

For more factual information on the Wright brothers, I suggest Russell Freedman's fine book, *The Wright Brothers: How They Invented the Airplane*.

A. G.

1064438557